Ingeborg Bjorklund's Red River
COOKBOOK

Favorite Recipes Collected by
Lauraine Snelling

BETHANYHOUSE
P U B L I S H E R S

Published by Bethany House Publishers
11400 Hampshire Avenue South
Bloomington, Minnesota 55438

Bethany House Publishers is a division of
Baker Publishing Group, Grand Rapids, Michigan

Printed in the United States of America

ISBN 0-7642-8187-9

Contents

Introduction

My goal in writing about the immigrants of Dakota Territory was to honor my Norwegian heritage by telling "our" stories and contributions to the melting pot of America. Little did my mother and father know that my experience of living on a farm with no electricity and using old-time farming practices would become fodder for these books. My parents felt bad that we were poor by the standards of the day. I see it as a great treasure.

So many of you have taken these people of Blessing into your hearts, and by sharing these recipes with you, I give you another part of their heritage and mine. For we are all a combination of the many people who have walked into our lives, and what better way to remember our histories than through the recipes we've been given. Ingeborg and Kaaren loved to feed their families and their entire community with food that not only sustained life but enriched the living. I love the idea that we are all drawn closer when we cook with these recipes. The traditions continue.

Thanks be to God.

BREADS

Julekake

Yvonne Oberg

No festive board is complete without this loaf.

1 cake Fleischmann's yeast	4 c. flour
¼ c. lukewarm water	2 eggs, beaten
2 c. milk	1 c. currants
½ c. sugar	1 c. each: chopped citron,
1 tsp. salt	candied peels, candied cherries
1 tsp. cardamom powder	½ c. nuts
½ c. butter	

Dissolve yeast in lukewarm water. Scald the milk and add the sugar, salt, cardamom, and butter. Stir until butter is melted. When mixture is lukewarm, add yeast and flour. Beat very briskly and well. Cover and let rise until double in bulk. Beat again and add the beaten eggs and the fruit that has been well-rolled in flour. Add enough more flour to make a stiff dough. Knead well. The nuts may be mixed into the bread mixture or pushed into the loaves after they have been shaped. Shape into round loaves. Brush the top of each loaf with beaten egg mixed with small amount of milk. Let rise until double in bulk. Bake in moderate oven at 375° for 45 minutes. This recipe doubles well.

Note from Lauraine

Instead of prepared yeast like we have today, Kaaren and Ingeborg used either sourdough starter or potato water that was left to sit until bubbles started to rise. Both sourdough starter and potato starter take yeast from the air when growing. That's why you use part of what you've started and mix water or milk and flour with the remaining starter, mix well, and let sit for a day or two until it bubbles again. Bread made from starters like these took longer to rise than our yeast breads of today. We are spoiled.

I achieved popular-parent status when I began giving my kids' schoolteachers a decorated julekake every year. I'd frost the round loaves with almond-flavored powdered-sugar icing, then cut green and red candied cherries in half and lay them in a circle on top of the loaf. I'd set them on a Christmas paper plate, cover with plastic wrap, and deliver. Most of our neighbors and close friends received the same. We had julekake sliced for breakfast on Christmas morning. Oh, so good. I've also seen the dough braided, but I never got that fancy.

Viola's Dark Bread

½ c. warm water	½ c. honey
3 pkg. yeast	5 tsp. salt
1 tsp. sugar	2 c. graham or rye flour
2 c. milk, scalded	½ c. wheat germ
1 stick margarine	white flour as needed

Dissolve yeast in warm water with sugar. Melt the margarine in the hot milk. Add the honey. Let milk, margarine, and honey cool slightly before adding yeast mixture. Sift salt with dark flour, add wheat germ, add white flour until dough is too stiff to stir any longer, then knead in additional flour until the dough is no longer sticky. Rise once. Cut dough into five even pieces. Let set for 15 minutes before shaping loaves and placing in greased pans. Let it rise in pans until doubled in size. Bake for 10 minutes at 400º, then 35 minutes at 350º. Turn bread out onto racks and glaze the tops with butter.

Note from Lauraine

If you can find freshly ground wheat flour, the difference in taste will be incredible, but this bread is so good as is, that's not necessary.

The more you knead the dough, the lighter the bread will be, but this is heavier bread, excellent for sandwiches.

I still remember Viola taking these loaves from the oven when we came to visit. While the kids played with the small toys in the drawer, she would tell stories of life when she and my mother were young. As soon as the bread cooled, she would slice it all and put the extra loaves in plastic bags in the freezer. Often I baked mine in round loaves for something different and added seeds to the top just before baking. Sometimes I used other kinds of flours, several tablespoons of molasses, and finely chopped sunflower seeds. Bread making is an art, and one that I'm afraid is disappearing.

Banana Bread
Mrs. Noah Winger

1 c. sugar	1 tsp. baking powder
½ c. shortening	2 c. flour
2 eggs	½ tsp. soda
3 Tbsp. sour cream	¼ tsp. salt
3 mashed bananas	chopped nutmeats

Cream shortening and sugar. Add eggs (one at a time), sour cream, and bananas. Add sifted dry ingredients and nuts. Mix thoroughly. Bake 30 minutes in a greased and floured loaf pan at 350° or until toothpick comes clean.

Note from Lauraine

My family loves banana bread. I used to go to the farmers' market and buy really ripe bananas by the box, then make several batches of both banana bread and banana cookies and freeze them. I have a friend who buys the bananas ripe, slices them in half the long way and dries them in the oven, set at the lowest mark with the door left open a crack. Milk shakes and smoothies are other great treats made with bananas. Having just come back from Hawaii, I can tell you there are many other kinds of bananas that are better than the ones we get in the stores. The squared ones are great sliced and fried in butter. But then what isn't good sliced and fried in butter?

Alma's Rolls

2 pkgs. yeast	¾ c. sugar
1 c. warm water	½ c. melted shortening
1 tsp. sugar	2 tsp. salt
1 c. scalded milk	2 c. flour
3 eggs	additional flour as needed

Dissolve yeast in warm water with 1 tsp. sugar. Add to cooled scalded milk, beating in eggs, sugar, and melted shortening. Sift salt in with 2 cups of flour. Add flour until dough is stiff and then knead in additional flour until dough is no longer sticky. Set to rise and punch down when doubled in size. Let rise again, and then form into rolls. Bake in 350° oven until browned. If you want to add poppy or sesame seeds, brush tops of rolls with milk and add the seeds. Or, when rolls are browned, take them out of the oven and brush the tops with melted butter. Let cool on a rack and watch them carefully, for anyone who comes through the kitchen will grab one for a snack. Recipe can be doubled easily. Use this recipe to make sticky buns or cinnamon rolls too.

Note from Lauraine

Every Thanksgiving our family, including married cousins and their children, met at one of the houses with everyone bringing something. I was always voted to bring Alma's rolls. One year a cousin asked, picking the seeds off the top of a roll, "Where'd you get these?" "I made them," I said. "Not with all the seeds on them," he said. "What bakery?" "I made them," I said again. Add an eye roll here and raised eyebrows. I'm not sure he was ever convinced, but he always ate his share, if not more.

TIP

To reheat rolls or muffins, put them on an aluminum baking sheet and cover them tightly with an aluminum cake pan. Set into a moderate oven for about 10 minutes. They will look and taste just like freshly-baked rolls.

Cinnamon Rolls

Edna Erickson

Soak 1 cake or packet of yeast and 2⅔ tsp. salt in 2 c. lukewarm water.
Add 2 c. flour and mix for sponge. Let rise.

1 c. sugar	2 eggs
1 c. shortening	1 c. water
2 c. flour	

Mix sugar, shortening, and flour together. Beat eggs and water in separate bowl and add to sugar mixture, then add all to the yeast. Add enough flour to make a stiff dough and knead in the rest. Let rise twice.

Brown Sugar Goo

½ c. brown sugar	1½ Tbsp. butter
2 Tbsp. light corn syrup	Melt in baking pan in the oven.

Roll the dough into a rectangle. Spread with melted butter and sprinkle with white sugar and cinnamon. Add raisins if so desired. Roll the long way and seal the dough. Use a long piece of thread to cut the dough and place rolls in pan of melted goo. Let rise again. Bake in 350° oven until browned on top. Spread wax paper on your counter. Take the pan of rolls out of the oven. Let sit for a minute, then upend it over the wax paper and let sit a moment or two before removing so the syrup can soak into the rolls.

Note from Lauraine

If you want to have any left for the next day, beat off husbands and children. Oh, and yourself. These are the best cinnamon rolls you will taste anywhere, well worth the extra time and mixing bowls. This recipe came from the mother of Annette Staatz, one of my best friends from our early married life on a dairy farm in Yelm, Washington. Edna would come from Williston, North Dakota, to visit and always made these.

CAKES

Apple Cake

Sylvia Worth

2 c. brown sugar	1 tsp. soda
½ c. butter	1 c. finely chopped raw apple
2 eggs, beaten	1 c. chopped walnuts
1 c. sour milk	2 c. flour

Cream sugar and butter; add beaten eggs. Stir soda briskly into sour milk. Add to creamed mixture. Add apples, nuts, and flour, and mix well. Pour into greased and floured 9 x 13 pan. Bake 40 to 45 minutes at 350°. Keeps well. Needs no frosting.

Note from Lauraine

I got this recipe from Bill Worth's wife, Sylvia, in Bemidji, Minnesota. It was Bill's favorite for his lunch bucket for years. Sylvia Worth is a shirttail relative of mine. This is the same recipe Ingeborg used for her apple cake. She could use either fresh or dried apples and sometimes added another apple. If using dried apples, reconstitute in warm water. Other fruits could be used in place of apples: pears, blueberries, Juneberries. Various spices could be added too: cinnamon, ginger, or nutmeg.

Barb McIntosh's Fresh-Apple Cake

4 c. grated apple	2 well-beaten eggs
2 c. brown sugar	2 c. flour
1 scant c. oil	2 tsp. soda
2 tsp. vanilla	2 tsp. cinnamon
½ c. nuts	1 tsp. salt

Mix together grated apple and brown sugar. Mix oil, vanilla, nuts, and beaten eggs, and add to apple mixture. Mix flour, soda, cinnamon, and salt together, and add to wet ingredients. Bake in a greased and floured 9 x 13 pan at 350° until a toothpick inserted in the center comes out clean. About 35 minutes.

Note from Lauraine

Barb and I met as lifeguards at Girl Scout camp during college. Ah, the stories I could tell. Using a friend's recipe makes you remember her all over again. Try this. You'll like it.

Eggekake or Sweet Cream Cake

1½ c. sugar	1 tsp. vanilla
2 eggs	pinch of salt
1 c. sweet cream	2 tsp. baking powder
(or substitute ½ c. butter)	1½ c. flour
½ c. milk	

Beat all ingredients together for 2 minutes. Bake at 350° in a greased and floured pan. Use a 9 x 13 pan for a thin cake or a 9 x 9 pan for a thicker cake. Can also be used for upside-down cake.

Note from Lauraine

Kaaren and Ingeborg used this recipe often. It can become a chocolate cake by adding ⅓ cup cocoa.

Icebox Cake

Eva Marie Everson

4 eggs, separated	20-oz. can crushed pineapple,
½ lb. butter or margarine	drained slightly
(butter is better)	1 c. chopped nuts
1½ c. sugar	vanilla wafers

Mix together egg yolks, butter, and sugar at medium speed for 2 minutes. Add pineapple and nuts. Fold in stiffly beaten egg whites. Place a layer of vanilla wafers in pan. Pour mixture in. Refrigerate for 24 hours before serving.

Quick Coffee Cake

Mrs. Rolf Brandt

¼ c. butter	1½ c. flour
1 c. sugar	pinch of salt
1 egg	1 heaping tsp. baking powder
½ c. milk	

Cream butter and sugar. Beat in remaining ingredients. Grease and flour an 8 or 9 inch square pan. Dot with bits of butter and sprinkle with sugar and cinnamon. Bake in 350° oven about 30 minutes or until toothpick comes out clean. Best served hot.

Note from Lauraine

We liked lots of butter and plenty of cinnamon and sugar. This favorite recipe of ours was a weekend special and one my mother used from the same cookbook when I was in my teens. Church cookbooks are marvelous treasure troves. I was given mine for a wedding present. It was compiled by the women from Our Savior's Lutheran Church in Bremerton, Washington. It's easy to tell which pages were used most by the stains and dog-eared corners.

Wacky Cake

2 c. sugar	¾ c. oil
3 c. flour	2 Tbsp. vinegar
6 Tbsp. cocoa	2 tsp. vanilla
1 tsp. salt	2 c. water
2 tsp. soda	

This can be mixed in the pan if you don't want to dirty a mixing bowl. Sift all the dry ingredients into a 9 x 13 cake pan. Mix well. Make three holes. Put oil in one, vinegar in another, and vanilla in the third. Pour two cups of water over the entire ingredients and stir. Bake at 350° until an inserted toothpick comes clean—about 30 minutes. Batter can be poured into ice cream cones for school treats, made as cupcakes, or divided in half for two smaller cakes.

TIP

When making cake icing or candy consisting of milk (or cream) and sugar, add one teaspoon of corn syrup for each cup of sugar used. Boil in the usual way. Your finished product will be much smoother and not so apt to become sugary.

Note from Lauraine

I don't remember who gave me this recipe, but it was our all-purpose cake. All three of my kids learned how to make this, and daughter Marie would tell you that you must include the sugar. We wore out several recipe cards for Wacky Cake, come to think of it. Perhaps I should frame this one—a reminder of many happy times.

COOKIES

Fattigmann

Mrs. J. Magnussen

1 c. sugar
3 eggs
2 egg yolks
¼ c. heavy cream
¼ c. melted butter

1 tsp. ground cardamom
1 tsp. baking powder
1 Tbsp. brandy
6 c. flour

Beat sugar with eggs and egg yolks until light. Add cream, butter, cardamom, baking powder, and brandy. Add only enough flour to make a dough that can be rolled very thin. Use rest of flour for rolling out on board. Cut in diamond shapes. Make a small slit in center of each cookie and turn one corner through the slit. Fry in deep fat to a light brown. Drain on paper towels. Sprinkle with powdered sugar.

Note from Lauraine

Ingeborg would have used lard for frying fattigmann or doughnuts. Fattigmann means Christmas to me. Like making other Norwegian goodies, do not try to substitute margarine for the butter, for that changes the texture dramatically. My mother made this treat, as did my grandma, Aunty Harriet, and other aunties. It was always saved in tins or Tupperware and brought out, along with coffee, to serve guests. I tried other recipes through the years but like this one the best, usually without the brandy. All three kids helped with the baking of Norwegian goodies—fattigmann, sandbakkels, and krumkake—before Christmas.

Sandbakkels

Mrs. George Loftness

1 lb. butter	1 tsp. baking powder
1½ c. sugar	6 c. flour
3 eggs	

Cream butter and sugar; add eggs. Mix baking powder with flour and add to mixture. This makes a stiff dough. Do not substitute margarine for butter. Press into forms and set on cookie sheets to bake in a 350° oven. Bake till slightly browned, then tip out onto a rack. Lift the forms off as soon as cool enough to touch. Store in tins or Tupperware with tight lids.

Note from Lauraine

The forms look like small tart pans and can be purchased through Scandinavian specialty stores or catalogs. I have seen various shapes but have the round fluted ones. They come in boxes of twelve; I have two sets.

This is a cookie that needs helpers to make because the dough has to be pressed evenly and as thin as possible into the forms. Our daughter Marie was excellent at making these too. I'm remembering the hours we—the kids and I—spent making Christmas goodies. Those were good times of talking, teasing, and snitching dough. I wish that for all families and gatherings of friends. Cookies automatically lend themselves to sharing, both in the making and in the eating. I've not made sandbakkels since Marie died in 1985. I take out the tins but put them back again. Almost gave the sets away when we moved, but one of these years I will gather some friends together, and we will laugh and visit and make sandbakkels again.

Berliner Kranser

Wilma Burner

3 hard-cooked egg yolks	1 tsp. vanilla
1 c. sugar	1 lb. butter
4 raw eggs, separated	5–6 c. flour (start with 4 cups)

Mix boiled egg yolks and sugar with a pastry blender until well blended. NEVER use an electric mixer—you would not be able to form the cookies. Beat the raw yolks with a wire whip and add vanilla. Add butter and flour alternately and mix with pastry blender first, then by hand. Roll small pieces into a pencil-sized strip about 5–6 inches long. Shape by crossing ends or by bringing both ends to center of strip and making a double ring. Then quickly pick up at point where ends cross and dip one side only into beaaten egg whites and then into sugar. Place on ungreased cookie sheet (sugar side up). Bake in 350° oven for 6–8 minutes until lightly browned. Enjoy!

"This is a recipe passed down to me from my mother. We have always had lots of cookies at Christmas. This Norwegian recipe is one of my favorites, though a little more difficult to make. I usually only make them for Christmas and special occasions, as they do take some time!"

Wilma Burner

TIP

When cooking eggs, wet the shells thoroughly with cold water before placing them into the boiling water. This will keep them from cracking.

Cookies

Best Ever Molasses Cookies

Viola Dill

1 c. lard	½ tsp. cinnamon
1 c. sugar	½ tsp. cloves
1 c. molasses	½ tsp. salt
1 c. applesauce	1 tsp. soda
6 c. flour	½ tsp. baking powder
1 tsp. ginger	

Cream lard and sugar, then add molasses and applesauce. Sift all the remaining ingredients into the mix, and stir. Cookies can be rolled out, but we like them best dropped on the ungreased cookie sheet with two teaspoons and smashed flat with the bottom of a glass dipped into sugar. Bake in a 350° oven until the edges start to brown. Cool on a rack.

TIP

To blanch nuts: pour boiling water over the nuts in a deep bowl. Let stand 4 or more minutes. Drain. Plunge nuts into cold water. Drain. Rub off the skin.

Note from Lauraine

Ingeborg had all of these ingredients, so her cookies would have been like these except she would have rolled them. But dropped and smashed is surely easier. I thank Viola for this large-batch cookie recipe. While she said these are great keepers, we never had to worry about that.

16

Grandma's Orange Cookies

Mrs. Carl Clauson

1¼ c. sugar
¾ c. shortening
2 eggs
½ c. milk
juice and grated rind of 1 orange
1 tsp. soda
2 tsp. baking powder
3 c. flour

Frosting

3 Tbsp. butter, melted
juice and grated rind of 1 orange
powdered sugar

Cream sugar and shortening. Beat in the eggs; add milk and orange juice. Sift dry ingredients together and blend into the mix. Drop by spoonfuls onto cookie sheets and bake in 350° oven until slightly browned. Should spring back if you touch the top of a cookie with your finger. Frost while hot.

Note from Lauraine

I have used dried orange peel in place of the fresh grated, but it is not as good. My paternal grandmother always had two or three kinds of cookies to choose from and was renowned for her cake doughnuts. I can still see her reaching into the cupboard for a big coffee can of cookies, followed by one or two more. She lived into her 90s, was a wonderful artist—especially with pastels—loved her garden, sewed clothes for me when I was little, and made innumerable quilts to give away. She crocheted afghans, slippers, and doilies and was active in her church all her life. She and Grandpa were church planters when younger. What an example she was of a godly woman, with a gift for welcoming people into her home, the coffeepot always on. I thank God for the relatives He has given me; the friends too. How blessed am I.

MAIN DISHES

6 Layer Dinner
Viola Dill

potatoes
⅓ c. rice
1½ lbs. raw hamburger or other
   ground meat
onions
carrots

green peppers
1 Tbsp. salt
1 tsp. sugar
1 quart canned tomatoes, undrained
black pepper

Place a thick layer of sliced raw potatoes in a deep, well-buttered baking dish. Sprinkle rice over the potatoes. Cover the rice with raw hamburger or any ground meat. Add a thick layer of sliced or chopped onions, a layer of chopped carrots, then the chopped green peppers. Add salt and sugar to canned tomatoes. Pour over other ingredients. Sprinkle with pepper, cover lightly, and bake in 350° oven for 2½ hours. This is good with corn bread. It is also good made in a Crockpot.

Note from Lauraine

Viola Dill was my mother's best friend from grade-school days. They kept in contact through the years by letters, and surprisingly, both families settled in western Washington about seventy miles apart. To their joy, visits and phone calls now supplemented the letters. After I was married and we moved nearer to her, she became my friend and mentor and another grandmother for my children. We loved to stop at Viola's house. The cookie jar was always full, sandwiches were made with her homemade bread, and for the kids, a drawer full of toys was right in the kitchen. Viola knew how to love, laugh, and play. We adored her. How I love to honor her memory with the recipes she shared with me.

Alma Moen's Baked Chicken Supper

Cook 1 chicken in 2 c. water in pressure cooker.
Cut up when done.

Dressing

1 medium onion	½ tsp. baking powder
6–8 c. bread crumbs	1½–2 c. milk (I use 2)
1 stalk celery	2 eggs, well beaten
salt and pepper to taste	2 c. chicken broth
sage to taste	

Fry onion till transparent (not necessary). Add bread crumbs, celery, seasonings, baking powder, milk, and eggs. Put cut-up chicken in casserole. (Grind skins if desired.) Cover with dressing. Pour on broth. Bake 1 hour at 350°.

Note from Lauraine

When I reread this recipe, I can see Alma in her kitchen. I only knew her as an old woman, but my mother moved in with the Moens when she was six years old so that she could go to school, since they lived close to town. The four Moen boys remember my mother as an older sister who helped with all the household chores. When I think of how hard my mother worked in exchange for the privilege of going to school, I remind myself to be grateful for my life of relative ease. We Norwegians come from strong stock.

TIP

To keep from crying when peeling onions, hold the onions under running water and peel with the root side up.

Aunt Margaret's Pasties

Crust:

1 c. lard (preferred) or
  1 c. plus 2 Tbsp. shortening
3½ c. flour
1 tsp. salt
ice-cold water (7 Tbsp. to start with)

Filling:

⅓ c. diced beef (uncooked ground
  will work too)
2 Tbsp. carrots
1 Tbsp. onions
1 tsp. salt
pepper to taste
diced potatoes

Blend crust ingredients and roll dough to the size of 9″ pie tin. Put first five filling ingredients into a 2 cup measure. Mix well. Fill measure with potatoes. Put filling on half of dough. Fold dough over and press together. Flip over and seal. Bake at 400° for 1 hour and 15 minutes.

Can be frozen after baking. To thaw and warm, bake at 400° for 30 minutes.

Note from Lauraine

One can also use a prepared pie crust, although Aunt Margaret might pass on again if she knew of such goings-on. She was my mother's aunt and lived in Hibbing, Minnesota. She came from Norway at the same time as my mother's parents—Bestemor and Bestefar to me. She used to make these for her husband to take for dinner when he worked at the iron mine. While they are good hot or cold, I prefer them hot. It's nice to have some in the freezer for unexpected company or a rush dinner. Do not thaw before putting the frozen ones into the oven. We tried warming in the microwave but didn't like them as well.

TIP

After cutting an onion in half, spread a little butter on the half left over, and it will keep fresh and will not mold.

PIES AND DESSERTS

Buttermilk Pie

Ann Applegarth

1¼ c. sugar
3 Tbsp. flour
½ stick butter
3 eggs

½ c. buttermilk
½ tsp. lemon extract
½ tsp. vanilla

Sift together sugar and flour. Add butter and beat until well creamed. Add eggs one at a time, beating after each. Add buttermilk, lemon extract, and vanilla. Mix well. Pour into unbaked 9″ pie shell. Bake one hour at 325°. Cool on rack.

"This is my Aunt Lela's delicious recipe, circa 1900 Louisiana."

Ann Applegarth, Oregon

Note from Lauraine

Ingeborg would have made this pie—or a version of it—because with her cows and her cheese business she had buttermilk on hand. They also enjoyed buttermilk as a drink.

TIP

To make a flaky pie crust, use cream instead of water.

Pumpkin Pie

Evelyn Wright

2 9″ unbaked pie crusts
3 c. steamed and strained pumpkin
   or 1 13-oz. can pumpkin
1 c. light brown sugar
1 c. white sugar
2 Tbsp. molasses

1 Tbsp. cinnamon
1 Tbsp. ginger
1 tsp. salt
4 eggs, slightly beaten
2 c. scalded rich milk

If canned pumpkin is used, stir and cook until thick before measuring. Mix filling ingredients in order given and pour into two pie crusts. Bake for 45 minutes at 350°. As a variation, stir in 1 tablespoon grated orange rind. Serve covered with a layer of thick whipping cream.

Note from Lauraine

When I was young, I always wondered why there was a cut in the center of a pumpkin pie until I saw my mother use a cold table knife to check for custard doneness. When it comes out clean, the pie is done. I tried other recipes and came back to this one that my mother used. While she would never have used a prepared crust—she made the best pie crusts anywhere—some available today aren't bad. I wonder if God has prepared a kitchen for those like my mother who so loved to cook and bake. Among many other things, she taught me how to knead bread and make excellent pie crust—some of my projects for Home Economics in high school. Her pies were always better, especially pumpkin, lemon meringue, and apple. How I miss her.

TIP

When taking pie from the oven, do not put it on a flat surface of a table to cool but on a high wire rack. The air under the rack helps to keep the crust crisp.

Rhubarb Cream Pie

Sylvia (Johnson) Skavlem

1 9" unbaked pie shell	1¼ c. sugar
2 c. finely chopped rhubarb	2 Tbsp. flour
3 egg yolks (save whites for	¼ tsp. salt
meringue below)	⅓ c. whipping cream

Mix all filling ingredients and pour into pie shell. Bake 10 minutes at 400°. Reduce heat to 350° and bake for an additional 40 minutes.

Meringue

3 egg whites
¼ tsp. cream of tartar
¼ cup sugar

Beat egg whites and cream of tartar in large bowl on high speed until foamy. Beat in sugar, one tablespoon at a time. Continue beating until stiff and glossy (do not underbeat). Spread meringue over rhubarb mixture to edge of crust. Bake in 400° oven for 6–8 minutes or until light brown.

Note from Lauraine

My mother always said the pies were done when they ran over. Our older son, Kevin, always asked Grandma to make a "rube pie" when he went to her house on the farm. The kids loved to go out and pull the rhubarb stalks, carefully tucking the cut-off leaves back under the plant just as she had taught them. I remember, as a little girl, searching out the most slender red stalks, chopping them fine, and shaking the bits in sugar—a special treat in those days. I now have a couple of plants growing here in my garden. Somehow buying rhubarb in the grocery store just doesn't work for me.

Apple Crisp

Mrs. Dean Miller

5 c. sliced apples	1 tsp. cinnamon
1 c. sugar	½ c. butter
¾ c. flour	dash of salt

Place the sliced apples in a greased square cake pan. Work the sugar, flour, cinnamon, butter, and salt together. Pack closely over the apples. If apples are too dry, add a little water. Bake at 400° about 45 minutes. Serve with cream or lemon juice. You can add nutmeg for a bit of difference. Once my mother threw in a handful of cinnamon candies, which added such pretty color and yummy taste. The recipe can easily be doubled for a 9 x 13 pan.

Note from Lauraine

I've used this recipe for years and passed it on to many friends. You can substitute rolled oats for part of the flour if you want more crunch. Since we lived for years in Washington State, apples were abundant. I still like Gravenstein apples the best. We had two Gravenstein trees in our yard during my teen years. They always ripened before the others, and nothing beats an apple right from the tree. This is one of those desserts that never has leftovers and is so simple to make. You don't even have to peel the apples if you don't want to.

TIP

When you make a double-crust pie, put a piece of macaroni in the top for the juice to boil up in, and it will not run out in the oven.

Apple Dumplings

Harriet Snelling

Peel and quarter as many apples as desired. Wrap each apple in pie dough, standing 4 quarters together as a whole apple. Put 2 tablespoons of sugar and a dash of cinnamon in center of each. Seal dough at top. Bake at 375° for about 1 hour.

Sauce

1 Tbsp. flour	2 c. boiling water
1 c. sugar	1 Tbsp. butter
¼ tsp. salt	1 tsp. nutmeg

Mix the flour, sugar, and salt. Add boiling water gradually. Add butter and cook 5 minutes over medium heat, stirring to keep the sauce from burning. Remove from heat and stir in nutmeg. Serve hot over the baked apple dumplings.

Note from Lauraine

This is my husband's favorite dessert, bar none. When we were first married, he said that since his mother served dessert after dinner or supper, call it what you will, he wanted me to do the same. For years I complied, which wasn't a sacrifice because I loved cooking and baking. One day I asked his mom how she had found time to make desserts every day when she worked full time and always had. She looked at me rather strangely and shook her head. "If we had dessert on the weekends, we were lucky." She raised an eyebrow. "Whatever gave you the idea we had dessert all the time?" Realizing I'd been conned, I answered, "Wayne said." She burst into hysterical laughter, while mine was rather chagrined. Wayne just shrugged with a not too innocent grin. It still makes me laugh. We no longer have dessert every day—neither one of us can afford it, middle wise.

PUDDINGS

Rømmegrøt or Sour Cream Porridge

This rømmegrøt cannot be made with our commercial sour cream because it is processed to prevent separation, which is so essential to the dish. If non-commercial sour cream is not available, make your own, as described below.

2 c. non-commercial sour cream or 2 c. heavy cream + 2 Tbsp. lemon juice	1 c. flour 2 c. hot milk ½ tsp. salt

Pour cream into saucepan and stir in lemon juice. Let stand for 15 minutes. Bring cream to a boil and simmer gently for 5 minutes. Sprinkle with ½ cup of the flour and blend thoroughly. Continue cooking for 10 minutes or more or until butter comes to the surface, beating constantly. According to your taste the butter may stay in the porridge, or you may skim it off and keep it hot in a separate pan. When no more butter oozes from the mixture under constant stirring, sprinkle in the remaining flour. Add hot milk a tablespoon at a time, stirring constantly until the porridge is thick and smooth. The milk is a minimum amount. You could need as much as 1 cup more to achieve proper consistency. Salt mildly to taste. Serve hot with butter, sugar, and cinnamon.

TIP

To sweeten cream that has turned sour, add ¼ teaspoon baking soda to 1 quart of cream.

26

Grandma's Rice Pudding

Jeanette Hanscome

This takes about 3 hours, but it's worth it!

⅓ c. rice	2 eggs
2 c. milk	½ c. scalded milk
½ tsp. salt	⅓ c. sugar
1 Tbsp. butter	1 tsp. vanilla

In a double boiler cook rice, milk, salt, and butter until rice is soft (about 1 hour). Let cool for 45 minutes to an hour. In a separate bowl, beat eggs, then add scalded milk, sugar, and vanilla. Add this to rice mixture. Pour into a baking dish. Place baking dish in a pan of water. Bake in 350° oven for 1 hour or until set. Cool and sprinkle with cinnamon. Serve warm or chilled. It is also good topped with jam.

"This rice pudding recipe has been passed around on my mom's side of the family since man first discovered that rice could be made into pudding. Well, practically that long anyway. My grandma, Margaret Rapp, made her rice pudding every Christmas, and sometimes on Thanksgiving or Easter, as well. Nobody could ever wait for dessert to have a bite, so it got served with the meal. Now my mother makes the pudding at Christmas. I have already been told that I will pass on the tradition once Mom is unable to lift the dish from the oven. It's great stuff! You might want to try it!"

Jeanette Hanscome

TIP

Add a few shreds of lemon peel to rice pudding for a deluxe dessert.

Note from Lauraine

Ingeborg and Kaaren could well have used this recipe. Rice Pudding is a longtime Norwegian staple.

Vanilla Pudding

LaDonna McCleish

1 egg	salt
1 tsp. vanilla	3 Tbsp. flour
½ c. sugar	2 c. milk, heated

Beat the egg; add vanilla, sugar, and a dash of salt, and then beat in the flour. Pour into heated milk and bring to boil over medium heat. Keep stirring so it doesn't burn. Bring to a very slow boil for two minutes, pour into individual dishes, and serve either warm or cooled.

To make chocolate pudding, add 3 tablespoons cocoa with the flour. Add bananas or other fruit, either fresh or canned, if you like. Another variation: Make chocolate pudding and add crush peppermint candies to the top.

TIP

Before boiling milk, rinse out the saucepan with a little hot water. It will prevent the milk from sticking to the bottom of the pan.

Note from Lauraine

Thanks to my friend LaDonna. I wonder if she remembers giving me this recipe. Ingeborg and Kaaren would have used this same recipe, both for pudding and as filling for a one-crust pie.

TIP

To make a quick sauce for pudding, beat up a glass of jelly—currant, quince, or any desired kind—and then beat into it the stiffly-whipped whites of two eggs.

MISCELLANEOUS

Mrs. Carl Clauson's Lefse

6 large peeled potatoes and 2 dashes of salt
½ cup flour (my grandmother stated this as a handful)
2 heaping tsp. shortening
¼ cup half-and-half

Cook potatoes. Mix all the ingredients and form into patties. On a well-floured surface roll out like pie dough, only thinner, and bake on a hot grill with no oil.

Note from Lauraine

Grandma made the best lefse anywhere. She said the less you handle it the better. Another rule is to rice the potatoes. My mother used to make ours on a woodstove top, well scrubbed. Today I use a lefse griddle. That's what Grandma used too. Most people use a thin, flat wooden stick to slip under the lefse and move it to the griddle, rolling it out from one side to the other. Lefse is very tender and tears easily. When it bubbles use the lefse stick to turn it, and when done, use the stick to carry it to the stack.

The stack is built with newspapers, a clean dish towel over them, and the lefse placed on the dish towel. Add each new lefse to the stack, then cover with a towel and more newspapers. Lefse dries out very easily. When cooled, fold in fourths and package in Ziplock bags. To serve, tear the lefse in half, spread with butter, sprinkle with sugar, and roll into a tube. Some folks add cinnamon, but my favorite is butter and sugar.

Potato Klub

2 cups all-purpose flour	2 tsp. salt
½ tsp. baking powder	Small pieces of ham or salt pork
10 medium potatoes, peeled and shredded	

In a medium bowl, stir together flour and baking powder. Stir in potatoes to make a sticky dough. Bring a large pot of water to a boil with 2 teaspoons of salt. Squeeze the potato mixture into 6 or 7 dumplings with ham or salt pork in the center. Drop carefully into the boiling water. Simmer for 45 to 60 minutes. Remove to platter with a slotted spoon. Serve with melted butter drizzled over. Makes 6 servings.

Note from Lauraine

When I was a child, my parents made blod klub using the above ingredients and adding the fresh blood from either hogs or cattle just slaughtered. Ingeborg would have done the same, never wasting a thing. I remember my mother serving the cut-up blod klub heated in cream with butter or bacon drippings. They would make a big batch and freeze some.

Snow Candy

Absolutely necessary: clean snow

Bring maple syrup to a boil. Keep stirring at medium heat until it reaches the thread stage. Pour in circles on fresh snow. Enjoy.

Note from Lauraine

In early days syrup was made by bringing a cup of brown sugar, a cup of white sugar, and two cups of water to a boil. Cook for five minutes, then add a dollop of butter and flavoring.

Ingeborg made this as a special treat, and kids through the years have enjoyed it. One of the advantages of living in cold country.

Spaetzle or "Poor Man's Dumplings"

1 egg
dash of salt
flour

Beat egg till frothy; add salt. Add enough flour to make a stiff dough. Drop by strings into bubbling soup. Cook several minutes and serve. You can add parsley or other herbs if desired.

Note from Lauraine

I use a fork and cut the stiff, floury dough in long pieces, dipping the fork into the soup. It makes a quick addition to soup or stew. This is an old recipe used for centuries. Ingeborg and Kaaren would have easily used it.

Aunt Edna's Homemade Ice Cream

1 gallon whole milk
8 eggs, blend in blender or beat well
  by hand
2 c. sugar

1 can condensed milk or 1½ c.
  whipping cream
1 Tbsp. vanilla

Take about 1 quart of the milk and warm on stovetop. Add eggs so that they will be cooked. Stir well. When cooled, add with remaining ingredients to ice cream churn. Fruits and flavorings may be added. Happy churning!

Note from Lauraine

The Bjorklunds loved ice cream, and thanks to their icehouse near the river, they could crank out ice cream in July and August.

Granny's Dill Pickles

Granny Robinson

3 qt. water	garlic
1 c. salt	dill
1 qt. vinegar	grape or horseradish leaves
medium-sized pickling cucumbers	

Bring water and salt to a boil. Add vinegar and bring to boil again. Loosely pack one- or two-quart jars with scrubbed whole cucumbers, 2 cloves of garlic and 2 heads of dill. Top with grape or horseradish leaves. Pour cooled vinegar solution to fill jars. Seal with lids and rings. Set in cool, dark place. Will be ready to eat in two months.

The same recipe is used for pickling in crocks. Pack cucumbers, dill, and garlic in the crock, layering with grape or horseradish leaves. Cover with hot vinegar solution. Finish with cabbage leaves and place a glass plate with a weight on top of pickles to keep them submerged. Let sit in a cool, dark place. Pickles will be ready to eat in about a month.

Note from Lauraine

Ingeborg would have made her own vinegar from apple cider. Floating a raw egg (in the shell) in the vinegar let the cook know the vinegar was of the proper strength. Pickling has been around for centuries as one of the ways to preserve food for the winter. Ingeborg and her family pickled meats too, along with vegetables and fruits.

Thanks to Granny Robinson, again from our years on the dairy farm in Yelm, Washington, I love making pickles. There is nowhere to buy pickles as good as homemade, be they dill, sweet, chunk, relish, or other various vegetables or fruit.

TIP

To take ice cream out of a freezer in nice smooth portions, use a kitchen mixing spoon and dip it in hot water a moment before taking out each serving.